PUFFIN BOOKS

It's Too Frightening for Me

Shirley Hughes was born and brought up near Liverpool. She studied at Liverpool Art School and the Ruskin School of Fine Art in Oxford. Since the 1950's she has illustrated around two hundred books in both colour and line. When her family was young she started to write her own picture books, which include the much-loved *Lucy and Tom* series. She won the Kate Greenaway medal in 1977 and in 1984 was presented with the Eleanor Farjeon Award for distinguished services to children's literature. She lives in West London with her architect husband, and has three grown-up children, two sons and a daughter, and five grandchildren who keep her on her toes.

Some picture books by Shirley Hughes

LUCY & TOM AT THE SEASIDE
LUCY & TOM GO TO SCHOOL
LUCY & TOM'S ABC
LUCY & TOM'S 123
LUCY & TOM'S CHRISTMAS

SHIRLEY HUGHES
It's Too Frightening for Me!

PUFFIN BOOKS

PUFFIN BOOKS

Published by the Penguin Group
Penguin Books Ltd, 27 Wrights Lane, London W8 5TZ, England
Penguin Putnam Inc., 375 Hudson Street, New York,
New York 10014, USA
Penguin Books Australia Ltd, Ringwood, Victoria, Australia
Penguin Books Canada Ltd, 10 Alcorn Avenue, Toronto,
Ontario, Canada M4V 3B2
Penguin Books (NZ) Ltd, Cnr Rosedale and Airborne Roads, Albany,
Auckland, New Zealand

Penguin Books Ltd, Registered Offices: Harmondsworth,
Middlesex, England

First published by Hodder and Stoughton Children's Books 1977
A lengthened edition published in Puffin Books 1980
This redesigned edition published in 1986
19 20

Set in Linotron Century Schoolbook

Made and printed in England by Clays Ltd, St Ives plc

British Library Cataloguing in Publication Data
A CIP catalogue record for this book is available from
the British Library

ISBN 0–140–32008–3

It's Too Frightening For Me!

Down by the railway footpath, quite near
to where Jim and Arthur lived, was a big
house. It was a gloomy old place with high
brick walls. The windows were boarded
up and the gates always kept padlocked.
Nobody went in and nobody came out,
except for a big tom cat, as black as a shadow.

On one of the gateposts, carved in stone, was the name:

There were spooks in there. Jim and Arthur knew this for sure because they had heard the ghostly screams.

Sometimes they dared one another to squeeze through the gate, where the bars had rusted away, and creep up the overgrown drive. Thick bushes grew on either side, dripping and rustling.

Round the corner, the drive opened out into a bit of garden where a crumbling porch tottered over the front door. There were little windows on either side of it with cracked panes of coloured glass. But Jim and Arthur never got a closer look before the screaming started, high and shrill.

'Go away, go away, go awayeeeeeee . . .' it screamed.

Jim and Arthur never waited to find out what was going to happen next.

'It's a spook!' little Arthur would say,
his eyes wide with fright. 'There's a
horrible witch in there. Don't let's *ever* go
there again, Jim.'

But somehow neither of them could
keep away for long.

Arthur had some nasty thoughts about

the house in his bed at night. Jim always pretended not to mind about that sort of thing.

One day in the holidays, when they were messing about on the railway footpath behind Hardlock House, they spotted a foothold in the high brick wall at the back of the house. Jim gave Arthur a leg up and climbed after him.

They both sat astride the wall looking
over some outhouses to the high windows
beyond.

All was quiet.

One of the windows was unshuttered.
Suddenly a white face appeared,
looking out at them! It was a young girl.
They stared at each other silently.
Then she beckoned, and was gone.

Jim and Arthur sat for a long time staring up at the empty window. Then they slid down on to the footpath and sat with their backs against the wall.

'Arthur,' said Jim seriously, 'that wasn't a spook. It was a girl. This is a real mystery.'

'Yes,' said Arthur. *'But it's too frightening for me!'*

Jim was frightened too, but he didn't let on to Arthur.

Jim's and Arthur's Mum had once read them a story about a girl who was shut up in a tower by a wicked witch. They thought a great deal about the face at the window of Hardlock House.

Next day they watched from the wall
for a long time, but no face appeared.
Then Jim noticed a basement door at the
bottom of a flight of steps, where the shutter
had slipped and a glass pane was broken.

Jim slithered down into the yard and tried the door. It opened! Putting his finger to his lips, Jim made signs to Arthur to stay where he was. Then he disappeared into the house.

Poor Arthur! He badly wanted to run home, but he couldn't desert his brother. After a long while, he too climbed softly down into the yard and, trembling all over, crept in through the basement door to look for Jim.

Inside the house was a long passage, smelling unpleasantly of damp. There were empty storerooms on either side, with high, barred windows which let in a little dreary light.

Up a shadowy flight of stairs and into a
large hall crept Arthur, expecting to be
pounced upon at any moment.

There were a great many doors leading
off the hall. Arthur paused. He heard

voices. He peeped through the crack in one of the doors. Then he opened it a tiny bit, and a little wider, and peered round . . .

. . . and there, as large as life, was that cheeky Jim! He was sitting on the floor, in a room full of furniture muffled in dust-sheets, talking to the fair-haired girl. He had forgotten all about Arthur!

Arthur felt like punching Jim but he couldn't because Jim was bigger than he was.

Besides, he wanted to find out about this girl. She looked rather nice, though a little

skinny. She was certainly not a spook.

Jim started to explain. 'This is Mary, and she . . .'

But at this moment the terrible ghostly screaming was heard in the hall. It was just outside the door!

In rushed a bony figure, all in black with wild white hair, waving its

stick-like arms about and gobbling like a goose in between the screams.

'Go away – AAAAH – go away – SHRIEK – I'll have no lads in here – AAAAUGH, gobble, gobble, gob – get out, GET OUT!!'

Jim and Arthur both dived under a dust-sheet and crouched there, like a couple of ghosts themselves.

They were trapped.

But Mary was speaking calmly.

'Come on, Gran, behave yourself. What about a nice cup of tea, then?'

It wasn't a witch. It was Mary's
Granny, but she was very nearly as
frightening. Peeping out from their
sheet, Jim and Arthur saw Mary take
her hand.

Slowly the screaming stopped. Mary
managed to coax the old lady down to the
kitchen and sat her in her chair. Not
knowing quite what to do, Jim and
Arthur followed, and stood about
sheepishly.

While Granny sipped her tea, still gobbling and mumbling into her cup, Mary explained that she was having one of her 'turns'. She always had them when anyone came near the house. She couldn't stand visitors, because she mistook them for people from the Council coming to ask questions and make her fill in difficult forms. This set her off in a screaming fit. She never went out, and didn't like Mary to go out either. Even the grocery man had to leave their boxes of food at the gate.

Mary told Jim and Arthur that she and Granny had come from far away in the country to be caretakers at Hardlock House. They had found the job through an advertisement. The owner of the house, Captain Grimthorpe, was never there. In fact, Granny had only seen him once, though a painting of him hung in the hall in a big gold frame. He looked very grand, with bushy ginger hair and whiskers.

We're too poor to look after things properly

Now he had gone off abroad and it seemed he had forgotten all about them, for he never sent any money for repairs. It was very worrying.

Mary was an orphan. She and Granny had only each other in all the world. Although they loved each other very much, Mary was bored and lonely without friends of her own age. School hadn't begun yet, and there was nothing to do but to sit at the window and watch the trains go rattling by. Her only

It's so lonely here, Uriah.

companion was the black cat, Uriah. She begged Granny to let Jim and Arthur come and see her sometimes.

Granny was reluctant at first, but finally she agreed. After this the three children often played together, and Mary learnt lots of new games. She was specially good at football. Sometimes Jim and Arthur even offered to help Granny sweep up, and went round trying to mend things for her.

One afternoon they found Mary and Granny both in tears. It was over Mary's clothes. She had to wear grown-ups' old ones, cut down for her by Granny.

'How can I go to a new school in these things?' sobbed Mary. 'All the other children will laugh at me.'

Jim and Arthur thought it strange to cry over a thing like clothes. But they had to admit that, although Granny had done her best, Mary didn't look quite like other girls. Her skirts were too long and limp, and her shoes looked funny. They decided to see what they could do.

That evening Jim and Arthur emptied out their money-boxes. They found that they had £2.83 between them. They asked their Mum if she knew where they could get some nice girl's clothes, very cheap. Mum was a sensible lady and didn't ask too many questions. A few days later she produced a large box full of second-hand clothes which had been given to her by a rich friend. Jim and Arthur, for their part, managed to buy a parcel of assorted hats for 50p at the local jumble-sale. Some of them seemed just a little unsuitable.

But when they arrived at Hardlock House with all these things, Mary was so delighted that she put on as many as possible all at once, and danced about the room in them. Jim and Arthur were so pleased with themselves. Even Granny cheered up a bit.

Hooray!

It was a lovely afternoon.

'I think Mary's my very best friend,'
Arthur told Jim as they strolled up the
drive the following evening.

'Even her Gran's not such a bad old
thing really, when you get used to her,'
added Arthur.

But a terrible shock was in store for
them. As they turned the bend, they
stopped short in front of the lighted

window ahead. Against the closed blind was the shadow of an enormous man!

Jim and Arthur didn't know quite what to do. After a while they went round to the back door and knocked timidly. Immediately there was a great noise of barking and the door was flung open by a fat man with ginger curls and whiskers, holding a villainous-looking red-eyed dog on a lead.

Behind him in the passage they could see Mary and Granny, clinging together.

'What the devil do you want?' the man shouted. 'I won't have boys knocking at my door! Take yourselves off before I set the dog on you!'

Jim and Arthur were too surprised to do anything but obey.

The next day they hung about on the footpath until at last Mary put her head over the wall. She looked unhappy and had been crying.

She told them that the owner of the house, Captain Ginger Grimthorpe, had returned suddenly. He was very cross about the state of the place, and was threatening to send them away. Then they would be homeless! What was more, he did nothing but shout at them, and his dog kept barking at Uriah.

Now Jim and Arthur were never allowed to see Mary. She had very little chance to play anyway, as she had to spend so much time doing housework and helping Granny look after Captain Grimthorpe. He was very demanding and sat about grumbling all day.

Poor Granny was quite worn out with all the work, and running up and down stairs.

But worse was to come.

Uriah had a big fight with Captain Grimthorpe's red-eyed dog.

He chased him all over the house and scratched him badly on the nose.

Captain Grimthorpe said that he wouldn't have that badly-behaved cat about the place any longer, and he locked Uriah in an upstairs room.

He was to be sent away to a Cats' Home in the morning!

You'll leave this house first thing in the morning.

Jim and Arthur looked very grave when they heard this news. They liked Uriah very much, as he was such a jolly good fighter.

'Don't worry,' said Jim, 'we'll save him somehow.'

He was a very resourceful boy.

This calls for some dangerous action, Mary!

Together they thought of a plan. Mary
was to get the key of the room in which
Uriah was imprisoned. This was difficult,
as it hung on a hook in the hall, just
outside Captain Grimthorpe's
sitting-room.

But Captain Grimthorpe always ate
and drank too much at supper-time, and
went off to sleep in a chair with his
mouth open. The red-eyed dog did the
same, stretched out on the rug.

Neither of them heard Mary as she slipped gently into the hall, took the key, and crept upstairs.

The plan was to put
Uriah into a cat basket,
and lower him out of the
window on a long rope, to
the boys who would be
waiting in the yard below.

It's only me, Uriah
dear, I've come
to save you.

Uriah was very
pleased to see Mary,
and greeted her
with loud purring.

But he didn't like
the look of the
cat-basket at all.

It was a terrible
job to get him to
go into it. At last
the lid was safely
tied down.

miaow!

Leaning out,
Mary could see
Jim's and Arthur's
upturned faces in
the dark below the
window. The basket
wobbled on its rope
as she started to
lower it. Half-way
down, Uriah decided
he'd had enough.

He started to turn round and round inside, miaowing and scratching at the lid. The basket swung about wildly, banging against the sitting-room window pane.

A light shone out.
The window was
thrown open, and
Captain Grimthorpe
put his head out,
peering into the
darkness. At that
moment Uriah's nose
appeared under the
lid of the basket.

Who's there?

In no time he had forced his way out and, clinging on for a moment with his claws, he made a great leap, landing right on top of Captain Grimthorpe's head!

There was a great uproar of wild cries and oaths, and a flurry of ginger curls. Uriah tore off into the night, wearing a ginger wig – and Captain Grimthorpe was quite bald!

Then a great many confusing things
seemed to happen at once. They all
crowded into the hall. Granny ran out of
the kitchen, throwing her apron over her
head and making a noise like a mad owl.

Bald Captain Grimthorpe stamped about, purple in the face with rage, calling for his wig. Mary was crying, 'Oh, Uriah, come back, come back!' And the red-eyed dog barked fiercely at everybody.

59

At this moment little Arthur stepped bravely forward, and said in a calm, clear voice:

'Captain Grimthorpe doesn't look a bit like his portrait up there without his hair on. I don't believe he's the same man at all!'

There was a sudden silence. Granny came out from under her apron and peered into Captain Grimthorpe's face.

'My goodness, I do believe the lad's

right. You're not the same gentleman as I remember – I can see that now, even without my glasses.'

'His moustache doesn't look very real either,' observed Jim, 'it's sort of coming loose at one side.'

Captain Grimthorpe's face flushed to scarlet, and so did his shiny bald head. Muttering something under his breath,

he retreated upstairs with his red-eyed dog at his heels.

'I always thought there was something funny about him,' said Mary. 'But don't let's bother about him now, the horrid old thing. We've *got* to find Uriah.'

For a long time they searched and called. It seemed hours before they heard an answering miaow, and Uriah came strolling up, shaking his back legs and pretending that nothing unusual had happened.

The next day Granny had some news
for them. Captain Grimthorpe had
disappeared! He had packed his things in

the night and gone off with his dog,
leaving nothing behind but a false
moustache on the dressing-table.

Of course, he wasn't the real Captain
Grimthorpe at all. It turned out that he
was the Captain's lazy brother, Maurice,
well known for his bad temper and
dishonesty, who was going about in
disguise to avoid paying his debts. Uriah
had revealed his secret. Neither he nor
his dog were ever seen again in those
parts.

Soon afterwards some people from the Council called. As soon as Granny saw them, she let out a shriek and threw her apron over her head again. But they were politely trying to explain that Hardlock House was to be made into an Old Folk's Home, with the agreement of the *real* Captain Grimthorpe, and that Granny was to be one of the first to be offered a place there.

Hardlock House was soon transformed, with curtains in the windows, pretty papers on the walls and flowering plants everywhere.

Granny soon settled down happily to
her new life, having her meals cooked for
her, playing Bingo and watching the
boxing on colour TV. She even got used
to the other old folk, although she
sometimes complained about them.

And Mary?

Jim and Arthur had grown so fond of her that she came to live at their house as one of the family, and they all three started school together when term began. Uriah made himself at home, too, without being asked. The food was much better than what he had been used to at Hardlock House.

Of course, they all visited Granny often, and kept her up to date with their latest news.

As for the ginger wig, which Uriah had abandoned on a fence down by the railway footpath, it hung there forgotten all winter, blowing about in the wind.

But when the spring came a couple of sparrows made a nest in it, and settled down to raise a family.

THIS IS NOT THE END!
(please turn over)

Now that you've read this story, you might like to try acting it in a group. You can make up your own parts, and add in any good bits you can think of.

You'll need at least seven people. The names with stars against them can be left out, or acted by the same people.

Of course the scene where Mary lowers Uriah out of the window will have to be imagined from the point of view of the boys waiting below.

CHARACTERS

Jim
Arthur
Mary
Granny
Mum
Captain Grimthorpe
Uriah, a cat
Captain Grimthorpe's red-eyed dog
People from the Council*

Old folk*
Grocery man*
    Costumes aren't essential, but it would
be more fun if you can get hold of:

A wig
An apron for Granny
Some clothes for Mary to try on
A tray with cups and plates
A cardboard carton with a lid for Uriah's
cat-basket

Also in Young Puffin

THE RAILWAY CAT

Phyllis Arkle

**Railway Porter v. Railway Cat.
Who will win?**

Alfie the railway cat lives at the station
where he's a favourite with all the
regular passengers. The only trouble is
that Hack, the new railway porter,
doesn't like cats and he soon has a plan
for getting rid of Alfie.

Also in Young Puffin

The
Village Dinosaur

Phyllis Arkle

"What's going on?"
"Something exciting!"
"Where?"
"Down at the old quarry."

It isn't every small boy who finds a living
dinosaur buried in a quarry, just as it
isn't every dinosaur that discovers Roman
remains and stops train smashes. Never
have so many exciting and improbable
things happened in one quiet village!

Also in Young Puffin

Milly-Molly-Mandy Stories

Joyce Lankester Brisley

Children love to read about this enchanting little country girl!

Milly-Molly-Mandy and her friends Susan and Billy Blunt live in a little village in the heart of the English countryside. They do all the sorts of things that country children enjoy – like blackberrying, gardening and going to the village fête.

MR MAJEIKA

and the

Haunted Hotel

Humphrey Carpenter

Spooks and spectres at the *Green Banana*!

Class Three of St Barty's are off on an
outing to Hadrian's Wall with their
teacher, Mr Majeika (who happens to be
a magician). Stranded in the fog when
the tyres of their coach are mysteriously
punctured, they take refuge in a nearby
hotel called the Green Banana. Soon
some very spooky things start to happen.
Strange lights, ghostly sounds and
vanishing people...

Also in Young Puffin

MR MAJEIKA

and the

MUSIC TEACHER

Humphrey Carpenter

"Music teacher? What music teacher?
I don't know anything about any
music teacher."

It's a new term at St Barty's and the
school is in uproar. Awful noises come
from Class Three, angry parents fill the
school and poor Mr Majeika is really
frightened. Why? A new music teacher
is coming who plans to start a school
orchestra, and as only Mr Majeika
knows, Wilhelmina Worlock is
a witch!

READ MORE IN PUFFIN

For children of all ages, Puffin represents quality and variety – the very best in publishing today around the world.

For complete information about books available from Puffin – and Penguin – and how to order them, contact us at the appropriate address below. Please note that for copyright reasons the selection of books varies from country to country.

On the worldwide web: www.puffin.co.uk

In the United Kingdom: Please write to *Dept. EP, Penguin Books Ltd, Bath Road, Harmondsworth, West Drayton, Middlesex UB7 0DA*

In the United States: Please write to *Consumer Sales, Penguin USA, P.O. Box 999, Dept. 17109, Bergenfield, New Jersey 07621-0120*. VISA and MasterCard holders call 1-800-253-6476 to order Penguin titles

In Canada: Please write to *Penguin Books Canada Ltd, 10 Alcorn Avenue, Suite 300, Toronto, Ontario M4V 3B2*

In Australia: Please write to *Penguin Books Australia Ltd, P.O. Box 257, Ringwood, Victoria 3134*

In New Zealand: Please write to *Penguin Books (NZ) Ltd, Private Bag 102902, North Shore Mail Centre, Auckland 10*

In India: Please write to *Penguin Books India Pvt Ltd, 706 Eros Apartments, 56 Nehru Place, New Delhi 110 019*

In the Netherlands: Please write to *Penguin Books Netherlands bv, Postbus 3507, NL-1001 AH Amsterdam*

In Germany: Please write to *Penguin Books Deutschland GmbH, Metzlerstrasse 26, 60594 Frankfurt am Main*

In Spain: Please write to *Penguin Books S. A., Bravo Murillo 19, 1° B, 28015 Madrid*

In Italy: Please write to *Penguin Italia s.r.l., Via Felice Casati 20, I-20124 Milano*

In France: Please write to *Penguin France S. A., 17 rue Lejeune, F-31000 Toulouse*

In Japan: Please write to *Penguin Books Japan, Ishikiribashi Building, 2-5-4, Suido, Bunkyo-ku, Tokyo 112*

In South Africa: Please write to *Longman Penguin Southern Africa (Pty) Ltd, Private Bag X08, Bertsham 2013*